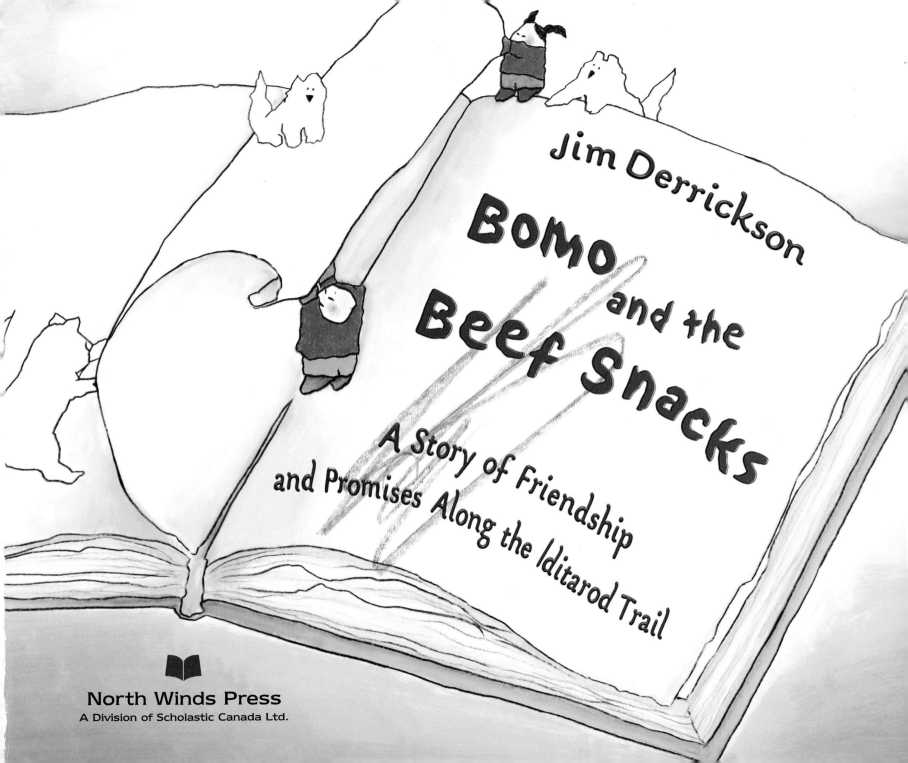

Jim Derrickson

Bomo and the Beef Snacks

A Story of Friendship
and Promises Along the Iditarod Trail

North Winds Press
A Division of Scholastic Canada Ltd.

The illustrations in this book were line-drawn in pencil and coloured with pencils on vellum.

This book was designed in QuarkXPress, with type set in 16 point Comic Sans.

Colourized by Chrissie Wysotski

National Library of Canada Cataloguing in Publication Data

Derrickson, Jim, 1959-
Bomo and the beef snacks

ISBN 0-439-98775-X

I. Title.

PZ7.D47Bo 2001   j813'.6   C2001-930475-7

5 4 3 2 1   Printed and bound in Canada   1 2 3 4 /0

It was late winter. Johnny and Rhonda got out their sled. It was time to run the Iditarod race to Nome.

"All ready?" the children asked the dogs.

"Woof!" came the reply from Bomo. "Woof!" said all the other dogs.

They howled for joy, ready to run to Nome.

They were all unlikely mushers. The dogs weren't even racing stock. Bomo himself
— the lead dog of the team — was an unnameable kind of dog, with bunches and
bunches of white hair. But for Bomo and his friends, none of that mattered.
What mattered to them was when the beef snacks would be served.

The dogs and the children had a special pact: that there would always be delicious beef snacks upon the long journey to Nome. They were the animals' favourite treat. Beef snacks were fun to eat, and they would keep their bellies warm along the way.

"Dash gee! Dash haw!" called Johnny and Rhonda.
Off the team went, on the long wilderness trail from Anchorage to Nome.

Through highs and hollows, across hills and ice rivers, flew the team of Bomo and the children.

Soon all the best mushers in the world were far behind the team as they hurried along to Nome.

Moose and Moose Baby came up to the trail to greet their friends.
"Woof!" said the dogs. "Hello, Moose. Hello, Moose Baby. Good to see you, friends."

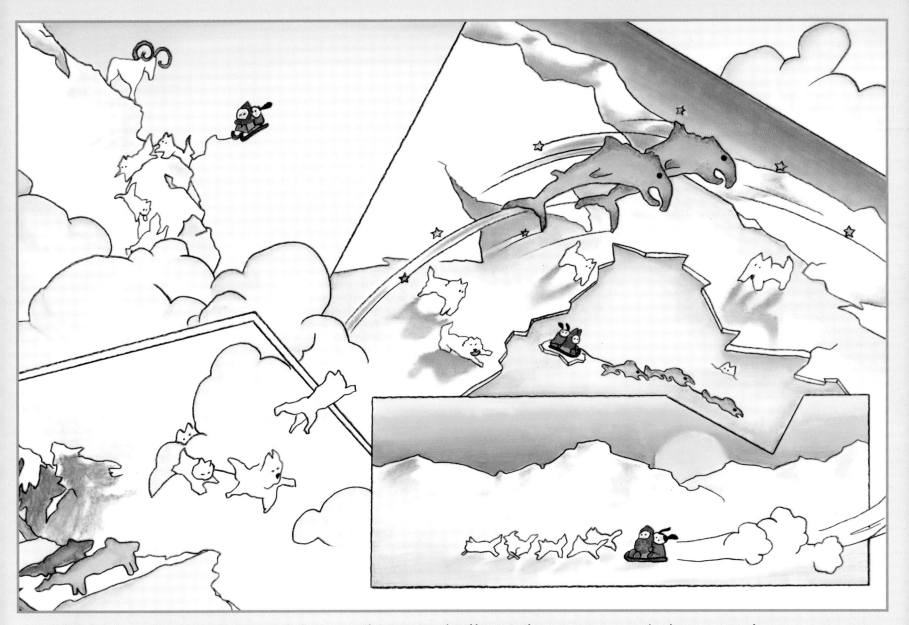

Bighorn Sheep came to the trail to say hello. Salmon greeted them. Wolves came to cheer on the team of Bomo.

"Hush!" Father Bear warned of his sleeping cubs in their winter den.

Nighttime came, and moondust covered the land. Owls came to say hello as the team made its way out onto the ice.

That night the children and dogs and wild animals had a party together, sharing beef snacks.

With the morning sun the team was off. It was time to hurry on to Nome.

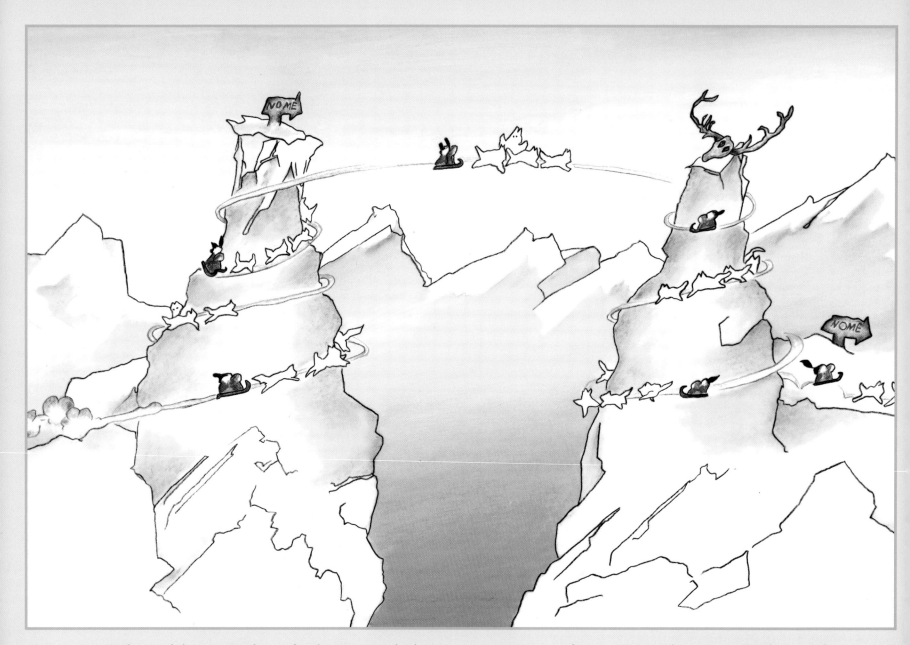

Whoosh! went the sled. Up and down mountains they went, hurrying through the wilderness.

They covered vast expanses of ice and snow on the long trail to Nome.

After a long drive, the team stopped for beef snacks. **Oh, no!**

The beef snacks had been left behind. Bomo and the team of sled dogs knew they could continue to Nome without delicious beef snacks, but the treats were waiting for them just halfway back to Anchorage. Besides, the children were bound to their promise: to make sure that the dogs would always have beef snacks to enjoy. And sharing beef snacks with their friends was even more important than getting to Nome or winning the race.

Why, it was the most important thing of all.

Johnny and Rhonda solemnly promise to provide Bomo and his team with beef snacks to enjoy, at every stage of the race. This a pact and we will not break it.

Johnny

Rhonda

In the blink of an eye, the team had turned around and was zooming back to where the beef snacks had been left. The other racers howled excitedly. It was the team of Bomo, heading back toward the start!

Whee! The team dashed to the old camp, enjoyed delicious beef snacks, and was back on the trail to Nome just as quickly as you may please.

The other racers cried out again, shaking their fists, as the team of Bomo passed by once more along the trail to Nome.

Lost in storms, the team followed wind-blown moonbeams through the frost.

They rode with the moon all night.

As morning dawned, they hurried down a rope back to the trail.

There was only one more stretch of wilderness left before them. Up, up, up the mountain went the team of Bomo . . .

. . . and down, down, down the other side they all came.

Soon the team was close to Nome.

The team of Bomo and the children crossed the finish line and were the winners of the Iditarod.

The judge made the big announcement. People came cheering. But the team of Bomo did not even hear the commotion.

Instead, the children hurried over to the grocery mercantile and scooted inside.

In the winking of an eye they popped back out . . .

. . . with delicious beef snacks to share with all their friends.